The Outside

Book 4

My New Normal

Sara Michelle

SADDLEBACK
EDUCATIONAL PUBLISHING

SADDLEBACK
EDUCATIONAL PUBLISHING
www.sdlback.com

Copyright ©2012 by Saddleback Educational Publishing

ISBN-13: 978-1-61651-784-7
ISBN-10: 1-61651-784-0
eBook: 978-1-61247-353-6

Printed in Guangzhou, China
0812/CA21201148

16 15 14 13 12   1 2 3 4 5

Day 14

9:00 p.m.

I think the shocking information from Dr. Jenkins was enough for us this evening. Cecilia looked pale, and my stomach was twisted in knots. Everyone else just looked drained. This man could be the answer to our prayers, or at least he could provide some answers. Millions of questions ran through my head. Why did this happen? Was this disaster worldwide? Was anywhere safe? And more importantly, what was next? According to Dr. Jenkins, more disasters were on the way.

There had been clues before the earthquake. But society had been too ignorant and busy to notice. Yes, it was obvious that the world had been in the middle of various crises. Why hadn't we realized that these "crises" were symptoms of something much larger? Theories of the apocalypse were reported like ghost stories around a campfire—only spoken of to arouse excitement or give a little scare. *That* wasn't reality. *That* wasn't anything to worry about. How wrong we all had been.

After Dr. Jenkins had finished describing his work, everyone in the shelter's kitchen sat shocked and silent.

You could hear a pin drop. Dr. J stood there awkwardly, his hands swaying slightly by his side. Renee's head rested motionless in her hands. Brittany chewed on her fingernails and stared at the floor. Henry and Michael stood quietly, unmoved.

I decided I should probably get the conversation going. I stood up and cleared my throat, awakening everyone from the spell of silence. I held my hand out toward Dr. J and offered him a smile.

"Dr. Jenkins, you're welcome to stay here. We have extra rooms with hot water and bedding."

He looked confused.

"How in the world did you guys manage this?"

I smiled and glanced at Cecilia. "Pure luck, sir. My girlfriend and I wandered for days after the quake. But then we decided to check this place out. We figured that if it was made to withstand the deadliest blizzards, then it must still be in working order. Luckily, we were right."

Dr. Jenkins nodded his head thoughtfully. "Very smart. Not many kids your age would be able to stay calm and think rationally after experiencing something like this."

I nodded my head and watched as Renee stood up.

"We don't have much here," she explained to Dr. J. "But we have what we need to stay alive ... at least for a while."

Dr. J nodded his head. "At this point I'm willing to eat absolutely anything. I'm just surprised everything is still working as well as it is."

"So were we," I said, sitting down across from Dr. J at the table. Everyone had dispersed from the kitchen and was doing who knows what. Renee stood over the oven, cooking. Cecilia, I guessed, had returned to our room. Brittany announced that Daniel needed a bath. The only people left in the kitchen were Dr. J, Renee, Henry, Michael, and me.

We decided now would be a good time to plan an itinerary for our supply mission. Michael, Henry, and I were planning to leave the day after tomorrow. We needed to come to some agreement on a couple of things before then.

Michael was insistent on the idea of digging through people's houses to see what we could find. For some reason that just felt wrong. I also wasn't too fond of discovering any decaying bodies. We hadn't seen a lot of dead people, certainly less than I expected, but I knew it was bound to happen eventually. My goal was to avoid it for as long as possible.

I personally believed that looking through grocery, convenience, and other retail stores would be more promising than the houses. The buildings were built to commercial code, which meant they were (hopefully) more intact. Plus the chances of finding a higher quantity of needed items in one spot would be much greater. Michael and Henry still felt like going through a bunch of houses closer together was a better way to go.

In the end, we agreed that we would be heading north toward LoDo: the Lower Downtown Historic District. Cecilia and I had arrived at the shelter from the south, so I had no idea what to expect in LoDo. But by traveling this way, we would pass by some of the richer suburbs, like Cherry Hills Village, as well as plenty of retail spots.

Survival supplies were the next issue on the agenda. How to handle the nights was the big topic. The weather had been pretty good the last day or so and much warmer than usual for this time of year ... but it was still the middle of winter on the Front Range. The weather was the one thing that you could never count on.

Renee had discovered some sleeping bags while poking around the storage rooms. Plus we would each have a box of matches and food to carry with us. I had no idea how we could prepare for every possible situation, but I figured we'd have to make due.

Day 15

10:00 p.m.

Yeah, I miss my old life. Who doesn't? I miss eating full meals. Junk food. I miss television. I miss my mother's smile. I miss my cell phone. Texting. Xbox. You name it. I even miss school. On a normal night, I would be working on my chemistry homework. Mr. Krieger was brutal with the homework assignments.

The Super Bowl would have been coming up soon. Cecilia and I would always throw a rowdy party at her place. Half the cheerleaders and football team would come. Junk food galore. The girls would gossip and only watch the commercials. The guys would watch the game out of the corner of one eye and watch the hot girls out of the other eye. I don't know if any of our friends made it out alive.

We spent the day prepping for the outside. Renee scoured the entire shelter. Michael, Henry, and I plotted and debated our course on a few maps. Brittany was keeping Daniel busy with silly games. Cecilia had cornered the doc. I don't know if she'd gotten a straight answer out of him yet.

I've been worried about Cecilia, so I spied on her. Quietly. She's been keeping a diary for a few days now. I guess it's a form of therapy. I wish she'd just talk to me. Anyway, I found this entry. It freaked me out. I feel so much pressure to do the right thing. But she seems so fragile. She's not the strong and independent girl I knew. I don't know what to do to snap her out of it. But something has to happen. Nothing is normal anymore. This crazy talk of weddings … Seriously? Our mothers are gone. D.E.A.D. We need to mourn, but we need to survive first.

I walked down the aisle in the October sunshine. My hair pins didn't hurt so much anymore, and the veil wasn't so irritating. I felt my two-foot train dragging behind me, along with the stares of the hundreds of friends and family that had come to witness such a blessed day. My heart that had only moments before been pounding at a thousand beats per minute had calmed to a slower pace.

I hadn't realized how completely ready I was for this day. The man waiting at the end of the aisle wasn't just the love of my life. He was my best friend and my soul mate. I'd known this for quite some time, and I was so happy it was finally time to make things official.

My skin glowed, and I felt prettier than I'd ever felt before. This day could not have been more perfect. My mother and Ryan's mother were watching proudly, with smiles on their faces and tears in their eyes. My gaze swept the crowd. But then I focused on my best friend, the man of my dreams, my soon-to-be partner in life. Ryan.

The aisle seemed too long, and the beat to the wedding anthem seemed much too slow. The closer I got to Ryan, the happier I felt. The idea of spending forever with him was no longer too hard to imagine. It now felt completely right. We'd conquered everything together; there was nothing we couldn't do. As I reached him, I realized I was finally ready for this. No more fear. No more questioning. Only excitement for what was to come. Our future. He held out his hand to me. When I placed my hand in his, with it I also placed my body, heart, and soul.

Day 16

6:30 a.m.

After struggling to fall asleep and feeling guilty about reading Cecilia's diary, I awoke and slowly adjusted to the morning. I felt refreshed despite my lack of sleep. I tucked away my doubts. I reached for Cecilia, but her side of the bed was empty. I jumped out of bed and walked out into the hallway, following the sounds of activity in the kitchen. Everyone was gathered; it looked as if I was the last one to wake up.

Before I could speak, Renee shoved a white trash bag into my hand, similar to the ones in Henry and Michael's. I figured this was our food rations for the next few days. I peeked in and was surprised to actually find some appetizing options. A small jar of peanut butter, saltine crackers, a can of beans, and two small bags of Doritos! My stomach growled. I'd never been so happy to see Doritos in my life.

"Renee!" I cried. "Where did you find these chips?"

She laughed. "I found a couple of things that I've been saving for emergencies. I figured that since you guys were willing to brave the unknown … well, you deserved a little treat."

I gave Renee a warm smile and embraced her in a hug. I found Cecilia talking with Dr. J at the kitchen table. At least she'd have someone to keep her occupied while I was away. I was sure she'd be bombarding him with questions the entire time, just like she'd been doing all day yesterday. I made my way over.

"Thanks for saying goodnight to me last night, babe," I whispered playfully.

She looked at me with those innocent eyes.

"Ryan, I swear I waited up for what seemed like forever, but I just fell asleep so quickly. I'm sorry!"

I felt like a jerk. I'd read her most personal thoughts, knowing full well that she was peacefully sleeping next to me. I had to choke back the guilt.

But Cecilia made me forget my sins when she blinked her beautiful eyes, making me laugh at myself. She was hot, no doubt about it. I kissed her quickly on the lips.

Our private moment ended too quickly. Before I knew it, Michael, Henry, and I were packed and headed out the door. We were organized. We were determined. My good-bye with Cecilia was brief. We both decided not to think of the negative aspects of what was happening, but to focus on the good ones.

Being back outside was a rude awakening. It was still cool, but it had warmed up substantially in the last few days. Days this warm were rare for January in Denver, Colorado. Well, they used to be rare. It was almost a refreshing temperature, and it felt nice to be outdoors again.

Although the temperature had changed drastically, the scenery around us had not. The city was a ghost of what it once had been. This side of town was usually one of the busiest. The shelter was located a relatively short distance from the downtown area, and we were near one of the most high-class neighborhoods in the city. But it seemed like a ghost town. The silence and stillness of it all was haunting.

Walking was difficult. The sidewalks were cracked and covered in debris. In some spots the debris stack was so huge that you had to backtrack and take a different route. I felt as if trying to get anywhere near downtown would take days. And how safe could it be? All of the windows in the high rises looked blown out. Some of the buildings appeared to be swaying.

Henry was the first one to talk.

"Can you believe all of this is even happening?" he mumbled, stepping over a pile of unrecognizable junk. He shook his head.

Michael scoffed but said nothing.

"It's still hard accepting it every time I wake up," I replied. "The disbelief hits me just as hard now as it did two weeks ago."

"What I want to know is," Michael finally commented, "is it ever going to get any easier? Are we forever and always going to be nothing but scavengers?"

Henry sighed and added, "I feel like we're in a movie."

We continued walking, avoiding the downed trees and fallen road signs and crumpled trash cans and other obstacles whenever we could, making our way through the most important scavenger hunt any of us had ever been on.

Day 16

3:30 p.m.

As we continued through the city, we all took turns explaining how our lives were before they were torn apart.

Henry explained how he'd begun his medical career and moved into a new home. His sister had gone into remission after battling cancer for the last year. His older brother was supposed to be getting married next week.

Michael had just moved back in with his mom. He'd been a runaway for the past few months and had spent his time staying with different friends. At the time of the disaster, he'd been in his room playing video games. His mom was in the basement working on a project. After blacking out from the quake's intensity, he said he woke up to the house being completely torn to pieces. He had to work himself out of the rubble. Once he was free, he searched for his mother. He saw her arms sticking out from a heavy pile of rafters. It looked like she'd made it to the basement stairs just as the house started to collapse. He was completely helpless; she was beyond help.

I gulped. I was relieved that I hadn't seen my mom hurt ... or dead. Although I knew that the chances of her being alive were slim to none, I am thankful I didn't have to see her hurting, especially if I couldn't help.

Henry's story wasn't as depressing. He was a doctor. He grew up on the East coast, went to school in the Midwest, and had just settled down in Denver to start a new life. He was alone when the quake hit and survived with relatively minor bumps and bruises. He and Michael had actually met the day before Jason found them and brought them to the shelter. The two of them hit it off and had stuck together over the past few days.

We rounded a corner and found a carwash tunnel that was still standing. The walls were sturdy and would provide a decent amount of protection.

We decided that this would be a good shelter for the night. Michael and Henry went to go search for tree limbs and other scraps of wood to start a campfire. I started setting up our camp for the night. We hadn't packed much, but I managed to clear some rubble and roll out the sleeping bags.

Once the campfire was started, the surrounding concrete walls and floor began to warm up. We decided to eat peanut butter and saltines for dinner. It was simple, but filling. We discussed our plans for the next day and decided to focus on promising houses in the morning. In the afternoon, we would search for any standing convenience stores. Although I still didn't like the idea of looking through the houses, it was the best compromise I could make.

After eating and chatting for a while, we grew tired. I longed for the bed back in the shelter. Once the talking stopped, Henry and Michael fell asleep. I thought about Cecilia and realized how much I missed her. I worried about her. Was she okay without me? I wondered if Dr. J had grown tired of the endless questions I'm sure she'd been throwing at him.

I could feel the hard concrete beneath me. My neck was stiff. I sighed. I was so thankful that we had the snow shelter to go back to; I couldn't imagine sleeping in these conditions. Every.

Single. Night. I was more than ready to get the day started so that we could get back to the shelter ASAP. After a while my eyes grew heavy, and I fell into an uncomfortable, restless sleep.

Day 17

11:30 a.m.

I walked cautiously down the path cluttered with toppled trees, fallen fences, blown-out windows, and remnants of typical backyard items, like barbecues and swing sets. I heard a faint hammering sound that was getting louder as I traveled further in that direction. I knew that leaving Henry and Michael this morning wasn't the best decision, but I figured I would get more done on my own. They were holding me up with their ridiculous plans.

As I approached closer to the hammering sound, my heart raced faster. I had no idea who or what I was going to find, but there was no turning back now. My thoughts briefly switched to Michael and Henry. I could have used their help in this situation. But my rash decision didn't allow for that option. What if the maker of the sound was less than friendly?

I walked toward the end of the alleyway. The origin of the hammering was around the corner. I was sure of it. The hammering suddenly stopped.

"Who's there?" a voice demanded.

My heart dropped. The voice was female. She sounded like someone around my age. I was silent. I had no idea how to respond and figured I should've probably prepared an explanation as to why I was pretty much stalking whoever this was. A few more moments passed.

"Look, I know you're there. So you might as well just show yourself. I'm not playing games here."

She didn't sound afraid or even curious. She only sounded pissed. I decided that waiting any longer would only make me look like an idiot, so I stepped around the corner of the alleyway and was surprised at the scene.

The chick, who had been demanding to see me, was definitely around my age. She stood there, glaring, hands on her hips. Her dark, cherry brown hair hung down, nearly touching her butt. Even from this distance, I could see that her eyes were a striking hazel. She wore a tight-fitting sweater that hugged her curves and skinny jeans that had definitely seen better days. Even in those tattered clothes, she was a knockout.

Just looking at her, you could tell that she had "it"—the type of girl that other girls envied and loathed. She was sexy. I'm sure Michael and Henry would agree, but they weren't here. Hell, I felt intimidated. That didn't usually happen around hot chicks. *They fell for me*. I stepped forward and cleared my throat.

"Hey look, I'm Ryan," I squeaked out, dismayed at how wimpy I sounded.

"Sorry to creep up on you, but I heard hammering and decided to check you … uh, it, uh … out."

She smirked. "So you crept up on me to check me out? Is that what you're saying?"

I blushed. Whoa. Definitely not! She was an attractive girl, yes. Very attractive. I felt like it had been ages since a girl had flirted with me, and I found myself stumbling over words. She noticed my inability to speak and laughed out loud. She had a heavy, heartfelt laugh.

"What do you really need from me, Ryan?" she asked, looking me in the eye. This threw me off guard. She had a playful spark in her eye, as if she knew some big secret about me that I had yet to discover.

I cleared my throat and lifted my shoulders.

"Look, I don't need anything from you. I honestly just heard you hammering and wanted to see who else had made it through the disaster."

She rolled her eyes. "Have you ever heard of curiosity killing the cat? I could be some psycho."

She was cold. But I had to agree with her. Not my brightest move. I decided that if I was going to get anywhere with her, I needed to show her a little bit of desperation. I sighed.

"Look, all I'm really asking for is a little bit of help. Maybe a friend," I said.

Her eyes softened, just a little.

"I'm not really the type of person to make friends," she muttered. "And quite frankly, I don't have the time."

I smiled. "Well, quite frankly, if you want to get technical, we have all the time in the world."

She groaned, turning away from me. Then she turned back, her eyes questioning. "You really can't take a hint, can you, boy?"

I crossed my arms over my chest. "Don't act like we're that much different, age wise," I pouted, playing around with her.

Two could play at this game. I pushed Cecilia out of my mind.

She walked up to me and stopped, looking me over from head to toe. I stood still. My jaw was twitching. We were playing a game of mental chicken. And it was getting uncomfortable.

"Well, Ryan. If you need a friend for a moment, explain how exactly I'm supposed to act. Do you need a shoulder to cry on? Want to sit around and play truth or dare?"

It's sad to say that her sarcasm only made her a hundred times hotter. I wasn't trying to hit on her, but she certainly took my mind off of everything else. I wasn't thinking with my brain. I bit my tongue and reminded myself that we were in the middle of the freakin' apocalypse. Girl issues should definitely not be one of life's priorities right now. I needed to focus on two things: supplies and survival.

Day 17

12:15 p.m.

"Forget the friendship issue," I said, throwing my hands up. "I just need some help. I was wondering if you knew a place or two where I could get some food and other supplies."

She laughed. "Of course I know of places. But why should I trust you enough to tell you where those places are?"

I turned my face a hundred percent serious. "Because I can help you too."

She laughed, and her laughter echoed through the alley. Once she collected herself, she paused. I could tell that she was making a decision.

After a few moments, she beckoned me to follow her and began walking in the opposite direction, toward another open alleyway.

"Follow me," she commanded, and I did. After a few more steps, she paused and turned around. "By the way, *friend*," she said, winking at me, "I'm Jesska."

My heart jumped. I wondered how in the world this girl had learned to play her games so well. She was the first girl I'd ever encountered who made me want to cheat. Jesska. Not Jessica. Jess-ka. I really liked it.

I followed her through a maze of alleys. I was a little turned around. The destruction here was similar to everything I'd already seen, except for one specific house. The house was small and needed major repairs. The front door was broken, and all of the windows were cracked or shattered. It had major structural issues. In normal times, it would be condemned. But this was the new normal.

We walked across the debris-covered yard, and she led me up to the front "door."

"Look, you can come in and explain to me what you need and/or want. I'll give you a bite to eat. I'm serious about this next part, though. If I find out that you told anyone about my house or the information that I'm considering sharing with you, I *will* find you and rip you to shreds. Understood?"

I laughed and nodded. I had no doubt that she was serious. But it was funny to hear such a small girl have so much over-the-top confidence. She let me in, and I was pleasantly surprised at the condition inside. She had cleaned out all of the debris that I'm sure had filled the house directly after the quake. The staircase had collapsed, leaving the upper half of the house unreachable. In the middle of the living room floor was a pile of blankets and two pillows. I figured that's where she slept.

I found myself wondering if she would be interested in taking refuge at the snow shelter with us. I tried pushing it away, remembering that it would only be asking for trouble. Jesska gave off the kind of attitude that Cecilia hated. She would call Jesska conceited. I decided that before I pondered the thought anymore, I'd need to really get to know Jesska first.

She motioned for me to follow her into what used to be the kitchen. The center of the kitchen had been cleaned, but broken dishes, appliances, and silverware were strewn along the edges. A small table stood in the middle of the room, and it was covered with food. I gasped and quickly ran over to check it out. I was surprised to find cookies, granola bars, Fritos, cans of soup, cream of wheat, and various other food items.

"Where in the world?" I gawked. I turned to look at Jesska, who was happily munching on a bag of crackers. "Are you going to explain where you got this stuff?" I asked, marching over to her.

She smiled and offered me a couple of crackers, which I accepted hungrily. "I told you I would," she said. "Let's go sit in the living room. That's the closest to comfortable we're going to get around here."

A few minutes later we were set up in the living room. We sat crisscross on the large comforter she'd spread across the floor. She offered me a jumbo-sized bag of animal crackers.

Day 17

9:30 p.m.

We spent the afternoon and evening getting to know each other over animal crackers, tomato soup, orange soda, and Twix candy bars. She explained that when she arrived here after exploring the streets for several days, the ground floor of the house was completely trashed. It'd taken her two days to get it cleared out, but she said it was worth it. She hadn't found any bodies. But she had no idea what was on the second floor. The thought of decaying corpses upstairs creeped me out, but I kept my mouth shut. She'd been living here alone for the past week or so, and for that I had to give her props.

As we continued talking, I could see her cold attitude begin to soften. She explained that she had pretty much raised herself. Her dad was a crackhead, and she only saw him every so often. He had plenty of bank and sent her monthly checks totaling thousands of dollars. She said it was nice for a while, but she had grown to realize that he was paying her to stay out of his life as much as possible. She usually lived with her mom, who traveled a lot for work. She explained that her mom was manipulative, unloving, and self-absorbed.

As I listened, Jesska's "coldhearted" attitude made more and more sense. She had simply grown up learning to not let anyone get too close. It was sad, but true. And it helped me understand her a lot. I decided that I should invite her to take refuge at the snow shelter. I'd just have to make sure that she was going to try and make a legitimate effort to get along with everyone there.

She offered to let me stay the night in her "house." Spending the night in the same room with a girl other than Cecilia weirded me out a little. It felt wrong, but exciting too. But in all honesty, where else was I supposed to go? I had no idea where Michael and Henry were, but even if I did, I'm sure wherever they found to sleep wasn't as comfortable as here.

As Jesska's breathing evened, she fell asleep. I found myself lying on the hard floor considering what a crazy life Jesska had before the disaster. I guessed that in some ways the disaster was a way out for her; it released her from alienated parents. I wondered how she felt about it. I really wanted to connect with her. She was so different from anyone I had ever known. Was there a chance for genuine friendship?

I hadn't given Cecilia much thought the entire day. I hadn't wasted energy worrying about her, taking care of her, or soothing her. It felt different. It felt exciting. It felt a little like cheating. My eyes grew heavy. The last thing I remembered thinking before I fell asleep was how I wished there would be a huge plate of French toast waiting for me when I woke up.

Whack! Jesska's pillow slammed into my face. And just like that, my dream about a giant Cinnabon and a deliciously creamy mochaccino was over. This was definitely not the way to wake me up. Back to reality.

I moaned and sat up, grumpily rubbing my cheek.

"What was that for?" I scowled. I hated being woken up quickly in the morning. I liked a slow transition.

"Rise and shine, sleepyhead," Jesska sang. I peeked up at her. Her hair was thrown up in a high ponytail, and she glared over me, hands on her hips.

"Get up, Ryan! I'm not kidding. If you're expecting any help from me, we need to get moving. And have you ever considered going to a doctor for that *horrible* snoring problem of yours?"

I blushed. I wasn't sure if she was being serious or not. Cecilia sometimes made fun of me for snoring, but I never really knew how bad my case actually was.

Jesska laughed. "I'm kidding. Get up though, boy, because we gots to go."

"Pfft," I started. "Don't call me that. I'm either the same age as you or older!"

She rolled her eyes and motioned for me to hurry up.

I stood up and stretched, thankful that I'd gotten a more restful sleep than the night before at the carwash. I followed her into the kitchen and was surprised to find a small plate of food set at the table.

"I went ahead and made you breakfast," Jesska explained. "Only because I figured you'd wake up late, and I wanted us to hurry."

I pretended to look completely shocked. "*What?*" I exclaimed sarcastically. "Jesska made *me* breakfast?" I put my hands to my cheeks in disbelief.

She rolled her eyes. "Oh, save it, Ryan. Sarcasm doesn't suit you. Chow down, and let's dip."

I sat myself down at the small table and began eating the peanut butter sandwich that Jesska had made. It wasn't the French toast that I craved (or the giant cinnamon roll of my dreams), but it wasn't oatmeal either … and for that I was thankful.

Day 18

7:30 a.m.

"Where are we going?" I asked, finishing up the rest of my breakfast.

She smirked and responded, "You're just going to have to wait and see."

Her games were starting to get on my nerves. "Is it a far walk?" I asked, praying that it wasn't.

She scoffed. "We're driving. I'm not *walking* anywhere."

I nearly choked on my sandwich. Did she say we were *driving*? I hadn't even considered driving being an option anymore.

"How in the world did you manage a car?" I asked in awe.

She shrugged her shoulders. "I put Daddy's big checks to good use about six months ago and got lucky during the quake. It was such a coincidence," she explained. "I'd just gotten back from running errands. I'd filled the tank up with gas. I went inside to put away the groceries, and then *Bam!* Total destruction. The earthquake." She paused. "The first thing I did after the earthquake was check and see if my Hummer was still okay to drive."

"You have a Hummer?" I belted out with a combination of shock and surprise.

She nodded her head slowly. "Isn't that just sick?" She smiled. "It's Colorado, man, four-wheel drive is the only way to roll," she said, trying not to laugh. "Of all the things I could have been, *should* have been worried about, I was worried about the car. Not my mom. Not my dad. Just me and my Hummer." She looked up at me and managed to give me a smile. "C'mon and I'll show you my banged-up piece of independence that we're going to be driving until we run out of gas."

I laughed and wondered why I hadn't seen the Hummer when she showed me the house yesterday. "Where is it anyway?" I asked, following her out the front door and into the yard.

She looked at me and squinted. "You honestly think I'm dumb enough to park a working Hummer in front of the house where any jerk-off walking by could have taken it the second they laid their eyes on it? I parked it in the back."

Not only was she hot, she was smart too.

We walked around the back of the house, and there sat this beautiful, banged-up, righteous Hummer.

It looked like it might have been white when it was clean, but it was now covered in mud, dings, and dents. The front windshield had a foot-long crack going through the middle. The passenger window was completely shattered, and the roof was dented from what must have been something heavy falling on top of it. All the doors seemed badly damaged and probably impossible to open. Jesska explained that the only way she was able to get in the car was by crawling through the passenger window. It was a miracle.

She did just that, and I followed her lead. But by doing so, I clumsily slashed my arm on a rough edge of glass. Pain soared through my arm, and I held back a yelp. I covered the scratch, hoping it wasn't obvious what had happened. I didn't want to be the wimp. But I could only hide so much when blood seeped through my fingers.

"Ew, Ryan! What did you do?" Jesska cried, looking at the blood that continued dripping through my hand.

"Me?" I exclaimed. "Your stupid car did this to me!"

My facial expressions must have been ridiculous because Jesska hooted.

Still laughing, she lifted her hair and removed the scarf from around her neck. "Here," she said, holding out her hand. "Give me your arm."

I showed her the cut, and she wrapped my arm with the scarf. It stung, but the pressure of the makeshift bandage immediately eased the pain. That was the kindest gesture she'd made toward me yet.

"Thank you," I whispered, looking up at her.

She stared directly into my eyes, kicking off feelings that I hadn't felt in what seemed like so long. The moment lasted longer than it should have, and I quickly looked down at the seat. This was not the time to mess around.

"Well, let's get going already," I muttered. "I want to get to this secret place ASAP."

Jesska looked away from me and put the keys in the ignition. The truck rumbled and spat but finally began its powerful hum. As we drove, I had absolutely no idea where we were headed, but I knew that it was going to be one heck of a ride.

Day 18

10:30 a.m.

Jeez, it was weird to have company and talk to a living person. Especially someone as h-o-t as Ryan. Big blue eyes. Ripped. I was *not* complaining.

Driving was difficult in this new landscape. The roads were covered with debris. There were potholes bigger than my Hummer. A lot of smashed and utterly destroyed cars covered the roads. The ride was bumpy wherever you went, and since the heater and radio weren't working, driving with company—with Ryan—was awkward. Plus it was freakin' cold without the window!

My social skills were not the best. Not that I'd had any company with me since the earthquake to practice my Emily Post etiquette, yeah, right! But now that I did have company, I realized that I had no idea what the hell we were supposed to talk about, especially after the charged encounter we'd shared.

Ryan was a good guy. I knew that. Sweet. Driven. Polite. Handsome. A typical mama's boy. Also making him (at least in my book) dangerous. Boys like him were the kind that I avoided. I liked the bad boys. At least with the bad boys you knew what you were getting. I had no idea what was going through my mind when I decided I was going to help him, but something told me it was what needed to happen. And now that it was, I couldn't regret my decision.

I'd already been to the warehouse twice. I'd pretty much figured out the easiest way to get there. The fewer obstacles the better. The weather hadn't changed much since my last trip. Hell, it's not like there was a lot of traffic, or *any* traffic for that matter. It was kind of cool being able to drive without obeying any of the traffic laws, and it made the trip go by way faster.

Even though it was faster, it wasn't a short trip. The Walmart warehouse was outside the city limits, normally at least an hour's drive. Going this speed I couldn't gauge how long this trip was going to take because the road conditions were always changing. The roads seemed worse with each passing day. Anyway, our destination was … good old Walmart.

Once we began driving, I wondered what we were supposed to talk about. Or if we were going to end up talking at all. The chemistry between us was charged, and I'm pretty sure it made Ryan uncomfortable. At least that's what it looked like from my side of things.

What Ryan didn't realize was that I wasn't usually so nice. I *am* the girl he met in the alley. I'm edgy and detached. I've always been. People take it the wrong way and mistake me for being some heartless bee-yotch. It's not true. It's just that with the way I've grown up, having your guard up is much better than letting people in. Who wants to get hurt over and over again? You just learn to put up walls. That's just how I roll.

I decided that anything would be better than this uncomfortable silence, so I started talking.

"So, Ryan, what was your life like before all of this?" I asked, hesitating somewhat.

I absolutely hated when people tried prying into my personal life, so prying into someone else's felt weird. Ryan looked up at me, surprised.

I focused on avoiding the crap in the road as he watched me. After a moment, he cleared his throat.

"It was good," he muttered, staring out the window. "I was on the football team. Cliché, I know," he said, glancing at me.

I smiled sadly, feeling bad that he expected me to be so judgmental.

He continued, "I lived with my mom. And we were really close. My grades were good. I hoped to get into a good college."

He paused and seemed to recollect certain memories that made him smile.

"My girlfriend," he laughed, "was a cheerleader."

I laughed too. "Okay, Ryan, that *is* a little cliché."

He chuckled. "I figured you'd mock our suburban lives. It all seems so hollow now."

Girlfriend? I looked at the road ahead and was surprised to find myself wondering about Ryan's girl. Did she make it? I didn't want to know, so I kept my thoughts to myself.

He sighed. "I don't know, Jesska. Maybe this is how my life was supposed to be all along."

"Huh?" I asked, confused. I couldn't imagine how anybody could think that this was how their life was *supposed* to be.

"I mean, maybe I lived through the earthquake for a reason. Maybe this is just how it was all supposed to work out. Fate."

How was it possible to find any good in this situation? I envied his ability to be so rational. I continued driving. The gas tank was only half full. I had no idea what I was going to do when the gas ran out for good. Most of the gas stations that I had seen were leveled. None of them had power for the pumps. I should have paid more attention in Physics 101. I sighed, thinking this would probably be my last trip to the warehouse.

Ryan had fallen asleep, so I was left alone with my thoughts. I tried figuring out what it was about Ryan that made me feel the way I was feeling about him. I would not have given him a second glance if he went to my school.

He was too normal. Bad boys were dangerous. Bad boys stomped on your heart. You expected it. But Ryan was a heartbreaker of a different kind.

I felt different with Ryan. I didn't understand it. And I didn't know if I liked it. But I took one look and my stomach flipped. I shook my head and wondered what this whole end of the world thing had done to me.

Day 18

12:30 p.m.

Just as the warehouse came into view, Ryan began to stir. He opened his eyes and looked around, confused. After a few moments he shook his head and laughed.

"For some reason, every time I wake up, I'm somewhere new. I wonder if I'm ever going to get used to it."

We pulled into the lot in front of the warehouse. When Ryan recognized where we were, his eyes lit up.

"Of course!" he exclaimed, grinning at me. "Jesska, this is brilliant! What in the world made you think of this?"

"My grandparents used to live right down the highway from here. I've passed this warehouse thousands of times, and it just came up as an option when I was thinking of places to go after the quake."

"Props to that!" Ryan said excitedly.

I stopped the Hummer and pulled the keys out of the ignition, deciding it was probably time to warn him about the smell.

One-third of the warehouse had been for refrigerated food: meat, cheese, milk, and whatnot. Massive destructive earthquake = zero power. Bye, bye electricity. Most of the food that needed to be refrigerated spoiled. The smell was gross, but if you breathed out of your mouth it was bearable.

Ryan didn't seem to care and was anxious to start collecting supplies. We crawled out of the passenger window, watching the edges this time, and I led him to the front entrance of the warehouse. The smell hit us the second we reached the front, and I gagged. It seemed to have gotten much worse.

"Ugh, that smells horrible!" Ryan said, pinching his nose.

I did the same and nodded. "Told you so!"

I led him into the huge warehouse. He gasped. His reaction was the same as mine when I had first come here. The inside of the warehouse was ginormous. I was really thankful for the skylights. Otherwise, we wouldn't have been able to see a thing.

The intensity of the earthquake had shaken boxes off their shelves, cracked refrigerators, and toppled pallets. Everything was a real mess. Although the place was trashed, it was obvious that this was the jackpot. We had just won survival Powerball.

"Whoa." Ryan breathed slowly, looking around. He dropped his fingers from his nose and looked at me with wide eyes. "Look at all of this stuff! How much of it can we fit in the car?" He looked like Santa had just delivered everything on his list.

I shrugged my shoulders. "We'll stuff the Hummer. We can strap stuff to the roof too. There isn't a lot of gas left, and I have no idea where I am supposed to get more. But I'll figure it out."

He nodded his head. "I'm going to take a look around. Do you want to split up for a while?"

"Yeah," I replied, starting off toward where I found boxes of clothes last time. Ryan headed to the food with a gleam in his eye.

I browsed around. There were sweaters, jeans, dresses, stylish T-shirts. If I was a normal girl in normal times, I would have died at the selection. Why was this a priority now? I didn't know why I should care about fashion, but I wanted to look good. I was seriously questioning my mental state.

After I'd collected and boxed clothes that I knew would accentuate the positive, I decided to take the stash to the Hummer. Then I would find Ryan. I carried my box toward the front of the warehouse and was surprised by the change in the weather. The wind was howling. I wondered if Ryan heard it. As I got closer to the front, I noticed an icy chill had begun to seep inside. My stomach tightened.

When I reached the entrance, I peered outside. My insides grew cold. Thick clouds had begun to make their way over the Front Range. The sharp wind was bitterly cold. I decided I would need to find Ryan now. I set the box down and hollered, "Hey, Ryan! I think you need to come here!"

"Hang on!" he echoed back.

A few minutes later I heard him suck in air.

"Whoa, Jesska, why is it so freakin' cold?"

I stayed silent until he reached me. I told him to look outside.

"Oh my God," he whistled, shivering. "That storm looks fierce."

He turned toward me, eyes wide. My heart pumped quickly. The weather had been so nice that I hadn't even thought about it being a threat. That sounded stupid, especially since this was Colorado. In January. Oh yeah, and this was supposed to be the end of the world.

I thought quickly. "I think we need to move the car inside. If the snow is heavy and it gets cold enough, we could have problems with the vehicle, and we won't have a way to get back."

He nodded. "We can drive around to the loading dock. There might be at least one bay for smaller vehicles with a ramp up into the warehouse." He glanced at the box of clothes I'd gathered. "Were there any *winter* clothes in the stacks you looked through?" he asked.

Huh? He noticed my girlie-girl fashion choices. Darn! "I only saw sweats," I replied. "Follow me."

We both collected fleece sweatshirts and pants that we could layer on to keep us warm while we moved the Hummer. As we walked outside, my blood turned to ice. Our situation went from bad to worse. I'd never seen anything like it before. I wondered if this was just another winter storm or a sign of something worse.

Day 18

4:30 p.m.

We climbed in the Hummer, and I shivered. Ice crystals were already forming inside the car. It was dark outside, and the gray clouds seemed close enough to touch. Heavy snow blew in through the broken window. I held my breath. We would not survive the night without shelter.

"Go around to the back. Let's see if we can find the delivery bays," Ryan ordered.

I did as I was told and watched the sky as it continued to grow blacker.

"What do you think is happening?" I whispered to Ryan, knowing that he wouldn't have any answer.

He shook his head. "I honestly have no idea," he sighed.

It took us awhile to get around back. The warehouse must have been as wide as two football fields and as long as ten. As we rounded the corner, I noticed that one of the back security doors was propped open. I parked the car near the ramp, and Ryan crawled out of the window to see if we could find a way to open the bay door.

I stayed in the car for a few minutes trying to figure out why the open security door bothered me so much.

Something just didn't make sense. My thoughts were interrupted when Ryan yelled, "Jesska, I think I've got it! Come help."

I crawled through the window and hurried up the ramp.

He was kneeling and messing with what seemed to be a small latch.

"Do me a favor," he said, looking up at me. "Go to the other end of the door. When I say go, use your hands to try and lift upward, okay?"

I nodded and walked over. Ryan wiggled the latch, pushed on the door, and hollered, "*Go!*"

I pushed and groaned. I felt the door loosen up, but it didn't open.

Ryan grunted. "It should open eventually."

We tried again and again. Finally, on the fourth time we attempted it, the door lifted open about a foot. Ryan jumped up, and together we were able to get the large door open enough for him to slip underneath. Soon I heard the heavy door crank clicking into gear. And in another second, the warehouse interior was exposed. And there was Ryan.

We slid back down the ramp. The howling wind was creating snow drifts. If we stayed out here, we would die. As we climbed back inside the Hummer, I remembered the open security door. I looked back over at it and gasped.

Five minutes ago that door was propped open. Now it was shut tight.

"Jesska, what's wrong?" Ryan asked, concerned.

I shook my head and looked at him. "You see that security door over there?"

He looked over and nodded. "Yeah."

"Well, when we pulled up, I noticed that it was propped open, like someone had done so on purpose. I thought it was weird. But look, it's completely sealed shut."

His squinted at me with a look that I couldn't read.

"What?" I asked, annoyed. "Say something!"

He looked back at the door and back at me. "Um, yeah. It was open? That would have saved me a lot of time if I'd known that. I could have just gone through it! Well, maybe the wind blew it shut, Jesska. What else could it be?"

I looked down at my hands. I couldn't ignore my gut feeling that something was terribly wrong.

"I just get the feeling that we're not alone here anymore," I said, looking up at him.

He turned pale. "Did you see someone?" he asked.

I could tell he was getting nervous. I shook my head.

"I think we need to get the car inside right now. It's our only chance to survive this storm. Then we can make sure that there's nobody else around."

He was right. Even if someone else was in the warehouse, our odds were better inside. Who wanted to freeze to death? Not me.

I turned on the car and drove slowly up the ramp; the wheels were spinning to gain traction as we reached the top. Then I pulled into the warehouse where we were completely sheltered from the weather. It was pitch-black inside. I flipped on the headlights and wasn't surprised that only one of them worked. It provided just enough light.

Ryan was scanning the dim-lit area with wide eyes.

"Jesska," he whispered, continuing to scan.

My heart raced. "What's wrong?" I asked nervously, following his gaze.

"I think you were right. We aren't alone," he warned, indicating a shadow to the far right.

My stomach dropped. Adjusting my eyes to the glow of one headlight, I slowly looked in the direction Ryan was pointing.

In the corner stood a large man with his arms folded across his chest. He stood with a smirk on his face, as if he knew some sort of secret that we didn't. He had large eyes that were almost too big for his face, and they gleamed brightly in the beam of light.

I totally freaked and turned toward Ryan, eyes wide with fear. He took a deep breath and looked back at me with a grim expression.

"Jason's back."

About the Author

Sara Michelle

As a high school student, I never thought that I could pursue my creative interests. But with the support of my family, I auditioned to attend an arts magnet program in south-central Texas. I'm so excited to be going to a school that lets me explore my right brain and harnesses my imagination.

Speaking of interests ... those would involve: singing, songwriting, dancing, reading, going out with friends, spending money, and—writing. I love this time in my life and plan to live it up while doing what I used to believe was impossible, writing and publishing books. One day I'd love to get my PhD in psychology—and in a parallel universe, I'd love to be an actor. My favorite food is ice cream; I could honestly live off of it 24/7. My friends mean the world to me, and I'd be absolutely nowhere without my large, crazy family. I can't wait to see what life has to offer, and I plan on enjoying every minute of it!

My New Normal™

The following is an excerpt

from *Book 5*...

Day 18

5:30 p.m.

It took me a few seconds after seeing Jason in the headlight to comprehend that it was *the* Jason standing there. I then realized that Jesska had absolutely no idea who Jason was or the potential danger we were in. Forget potential. We were in danger. Jason had promised that he would be back, and unfortunately, it looked like he kept his promises. Just my luck.

"Who the hell?" Jesska asked, glancing at me nervously. The headlight was the only source of light available in the warehouse, and I was determined to keep it shining bright.

"Jesska," I whispered. "I need you to stay in the car. And whatever you do, don't let the headlight go dark. Okay?"

I looked into her eyes and saw confusion, fear, and just a little sass. I knew she would have my back.

"Who *is* Jason? You *know* him?" she muttered frantically.

I nodded. "He was with us in the shelter. We kicked him out because he was a threat. Dangerous. Possibly crazy. It's a long story."

I slowly climbed through the passenger side window out onto the concrete floor. I walked forward, pulling my shoulders back, trying to make myself look as built as possible.

The headlight gave Jason an eerie glow. He looked like a specter. Truly creepy. My heart raced as I realized how unprepared I was for this confrontation. If this was war, my chances were slim to none. We both stared at each other before a slow smirk spread across his face.

"Rrry-aan!" he boomed.